Ma'an's Journey

Series Name: The Fish and the Coin

This is a work of fiction. Names, places, incidents, and characters are the product of the Author's imaginative mind or are used fictitiously, unless there has been clear consent from individuals. Any resemblance to actual persons, with exception to the Bible, living or dead, events, or locales is entirely coincidental.

Author's contact details:
Email: gloire041988@gmail.com
Instagram: Gloire777
Facebook: Gloire Emmanuel Ndongala

Published by,
Gloire Emmanuel Ndongala

ISBN: 978-1-7334909-5-5 (Paperback)
ISBN: 978-1-7334909-4-8 (Ebook)
ISBN: 978-1-7334909-6-2 (Audiobook)

For the Glory of God

Ma'an's Journey

The Fish and the Coin

Table of Contents

Chapter 1

Different Families

Ma'an

The *Sea of Galilee* is one of the most popular seas in the whole world. Alright, it's not really a sea, but the name sounds a lot better than the *Lake of Galilee*, so we made an exception. The Sea of Galilee is my home. I would describe life here as grand, maybe it's because it's all I've ever known. There is a hierarchy here among us fish. The best fish live closer to the surface where food is plentiful, while the not-so-popular fish live on the bottom, where food is scarce.

There are three different families that live down in the bottom, in my neighborhood. Some of the families are broken up into different clans. The Cyprinid Family is known for their massive size and barbels, which look like handlebar mustaches. This gives them the nickname *Biny*. They are broken up into three clans: the *Longiceps* that have massive bellies, the *Canis* that have bigger heads, and their distant cousins, the *Kinneret* sardine who are so different from their cousins that over time they became their own family—they are known for their tiny stature. Although these clans are related, they don't all get along. They each stay with their own, reluctantly helping each other, never visiting one another, and always competing against each other.

Last but not least—my family—the Cichlidae family. We have two clans in my neighborhood: the *Tristramella Simonis*[i] shoal known for their different shades of purple scales, and my clan the *Sarotherodon*[ii]. We're called the Musht, but watch your mouth when you're pronouncing it. We're known for our stylish mohawks and different colors in our scales[iii].

Cyprinid Family

Distant

Longiceps

Canis

Kineret

Cichlidae

Simonis

Musht

For the most part, each family sticks to its own kind. Nevertheless, once in a while, fights break out between the different families. What are the fights about, you might ask? Well, let me tell you.

The Sea first belonged to my great, great, great, great. . . You get the idea. Anyway, he was my many greats Grandpa Galilee. Grandpa Galilee was chosen, handpicked, by the Creator of the sea to be the father of all the fish that "*believe*"—whatever that means. To this day, our shoal defends our sea from everyone else.

All the fish down here live in Rocky Cove. The name Rocky Cove comes from the mounds of underwater rocks. Some are as large as boulders, others are as small as pebbles, and they all surround our community. Certain places have sand and underwater grass that sprout up through the rocks.

We all grew up hearing about prophecies of things to come. One of these prophecies claimed, "One day, there will be a ManGod that wields the power to calm the sea, tame the storms, and walk on water." The prophecy went on to say, "The fish that sees him doing these things will carry a coin out of the sea." This prophecy had been passed on for many generations, but no one really believes in this stuff. I mean, I'd seen plenty of men fall into the water and not one was ever able to walk on water. We had plenty of ships and boats become part of our domain that were crushed by the storms. Not one person was able to calm the storm, so I thought these were just ancient stories the old fish told us to pass both time and history to the next generation.

Not to mention the fact that humans were always trying to eat us, so why would we bring a coin outside the sea? It goes without saying that a lot of this fishery came from the Seers, the ones who know the unknown. Even though I'd never seen them, I was told they exist.

Before I go on, let me formally introduce myself. My name is Ma'an (mah'-an)[iv]. As I already told you, I am a Musht of the Sarotherodon shoal. Each shoal is supposed to stick to their own kind, but my two best friends happen to be from the other families. From the Biny Longiceps shoal comes my friend, Alziwaq (Al-zi-waq-o)[v], and from the Kinneret shoal is my friend Tsel' (Ts-él)[vi].

You see, I don't really see things the way my tribe sees them. I think if Grandpa Galilee was supposed to be a father to many fish, wouldn't that mean we are all supposed to be a family? This question remains unanswered because we don't talk about this amongst the Elders of our tribe. In fact, if anyone found out about my friends, I could experience death on a wood board. I had been told it's an excruciating way to die. The Elders would come together with parts of leftover nets that had been lost by humans. Then they tie you to a board from one of the ships that crashed. As you proceed to float on the surface, you become bird sushi.

Despite all the dangers, I still refused to give up my friends. How I met my friends could not have been an accident. You see, when I was born my mom had a mouth full of kids. Literally, we all pretty much lived in her mouth and were supposed to always stay close. We were not supposed to drift away from our cove, but I've always had a heart for adventure. I loved to explore. One day when our mom released us, she told us not to go far, but there was a sunken boat several fins from where I was and I couldn't help but go explore it.

My brothers and sisters warned me, but I told them I could take care of myself. I remember thinking to myself, *If I can see the boat, I can see them from the boat.*

I ventured closer. Closer. Closer to the boat, further and further from my family. I couldn't hear them anymore. I admit, I was a little scared realizing I was so far away.

"Hey!" I heard a deep yell suddenly. I froze, startled! The voice continued speaking, "What are you doing by my boat?"

"I'm sorry, I didn't know this was your boat," I replied.

The voice spoke again, "You're lucky I'm feeling gracious today or I'd take your life! Now go back to where you came from Mu!"

When I heard him say 'Mu,' I knew it wasn't a big scary fish. Only the Kinneret family couldn't pronounce the 'sht' in our name—it was forbidden for their clan. I spoke up, "Show yourself, you midget fish!" The one thing you never call a Kinneret fish is anything that makes fun of their stature.

I heard a loud scream heading toward me from the Kinneret fish, "AAAAAAHHHHHHHHHH!!!!!"

I braced myself for the impending impact. Right before he hit me, another fish came between us. He had a very soft, but cool voice as he proclaimed, "Yo! This is my boat!" It was a little fish from the Biny family. It wasn't a grown up, or else we'd be dead.

We were at a standstill and we heard...nothing! Absolutely nothing! My scales started to feel weird as if we were being watched as we floated in silence. Then I saw it! No one had ever seen one and lived to tell. It had long string-like barbels coming from its mouth.

"Swim!!!" I yelled as I frantically swam toward the boat. The other two fish followed me and we started weaving through the boat. We found some small cracks and swam inside. It was dark and eerie. We could hear it above us. It was a loud noise, "CRRRROAK CRRRRROAK!" The sound echoed above us.

We waited silently and held our water for what seemed like an eternity. We tried to peep through the cracks in the boat in hopes of seeing if it was still out there. When we felt like it was gone, we all let out a sigh of relief. We looked at each other for the first time and laughed. I was the first to speak up, "My name is Ma'an."

The small Biny Kinneret fish was the next to speak, in his deep voice, "Mine is Tsel'."

"I'm Alziwaq," said the Biny Longicep fish in his smooth, calm tone.

The uncertainty of our situation that day was overshadowed by our new friendship. From that day forward, we were best friends. That boat became our place where we would secretly meet up. There, we vowed to never tell anyone about our 'secret club' because we knew if our families found out about it, it would be the end of our friendship, and possibly our lives.

Chapter 2

School

Ma'an

Although our families couldn't stand each other, they still had certain rules they agreed upon. First, no matter what, if we saw a human, we had to alert each other. Second, the grown-ups also agreed that the only way to keep the fishlings safe was by educating them on ways to survive together. The final rule was that no one was allowed to go beyond the sunken boats. The boats resided about 1,000 fins from our vicinity and we all wanted to explore them, even though the grown-ups couldn't seem to understand why.

If you were a larvae (baby fish), a fry (child fish), or a fingerling (teen fish)[vii], you were not to venture to the boats at all. Unfortunately, we were still fingerlings so it was forbidden. . . But we did it anyway. Our school was located in the center of our communities, where there were many pebbles and sand everywhere. Each classroom was separated by large rocks. Depending on the size of the fish, we used rocks that we could float behind and still see over for our tables. Our teachers generally taught our class in front of a giant stone called the Stone of Knowledge. They also had a rock desk they would lecture from on occasion.

If you were to view the classes from above, you would see our formation resembled the image of a capital T from the Latin Alphabet. The line that capitalized the T would be where the teaching stone sat, and the center line going down on the T would be the dividing wall. There was a total of three T formations; each T consisting of two classes.

In school we learned basic survival skills. Our teachers were members from each family. The first class of the day was how nibbling on food could save your life. Apparently, humans had a way of hiding sharp objects in our food so that when we swallowed it, they could catch us! This is how a lot of glutton fish (fish that love to eat even after they are full), are taken and ultimately die. My dad was one of them.

School
Desk
Teacher Desk

My dad, who was an amazing Musht, loved to eat. One day, he saw some food floating in the distance. Upon reaching the food, he couldn't help himself—he lost all the teachings he had been given and refused to nibble. Instead, he went full force toward the food and we never saw him again. As far as fish are concerned, nibbling is pretty important.

In the next class, we learned how to read and write bubbles. This class was my favorite. It was taught by the only teacher who truly knew about the prophecy. His name was MoAwesome. He was part of the Biny clan. My mom told me not to listen to his gibberfish about what lies beyond the shipwrecks. According to her, he spoke to her once and sounded very incoherent. I had so many questions for him though! Also, I heard he eats fingerlings. Instead of scaring me though, it just made me want to talk to him more.

I heard that one time a student stayed after school to talk to him and he was never seen again. The language he taught is an ancient language that none of us use anymore, but apparently the prophecy was written by an ancient Betta who passed down the technique of speaking in bubbles to our Great Elders. We practiced it in class just in case one of us happened to be the one who fulfills the prophecy.

The Betta language goes like this: the biggest bubble means '*God*'. Two bubbles next to each other side by side in a line means '*man*'. Three bubbles in a row means '*fish*'. The prophecy told through bubbles looks like this: the biggest bubble and under it is two bubbles going down, meaning '*God will come down*'. Then, under that are bubbles in the shape of a cross which means '*and will become*' and under it are two bubbles side by side in a line which means '*man*'.

- Water
OOO - fish
- seeing
- will take
- coin
- out
- Water
OO - men
- He
OO - Two Bubbles Side by side = Ma
Biggest Bubble = GOD
OOO - Three bubbles in a row = FISH
- and will become
GOD WILL COME DOWN
BETA
→ Will calm bringing peace
← Storm
OO ← Godman

In the language of bubbles, small bubbles that make a big circle is the symbol for '*water*'. Little bubbles that make a square mean '*clouds*.' Then there are small bubbles making a triangle which means '*wind*'. In the prophecy when you put the square and the triangle made by little bubbles all inside the big circle made also of little bubbles going in a circular line you get the word '*storm*.'

Next, there is a bubble within a bubble meaning '*He*,' followed by five bubbles in a perfect line meaning '*will calm*' or '*bring peace,*' followed by bubbles forming a square and a triangle inside the circle of bubbles meaning '*storm*.' Then there is the biggest bubble and to the right of it are two bubbles in a row meaning '*God man*' followed by bubbles in a row but rotating up and down, six of them, meaning '*walking*.' After this are small bubbles making a circle meaning '*water*.' This is followed by three bubbles in a row meaning '*fish*.'

Then this is followed by two bubbles overlapping side by side which means 'seeing.' After this are little bubbles in a U-shape which means '*will take*,' followed by three bubbles inside each other meaning '*coin*.' This is followed by little bubbles making the shape of an *N* from the Latin Alphabet meaning '*out*.' Lastly the little bubbles making a circle meaning '*water*.' Put it all together and it says, "*God will come down and become a man and he will calm the storms and walk on water. The fish that sees him calming the storm and walking on water will carry a coin out of the water.*"

It was all a bunch of gibberfish, if you ask me. Very confusing and hard to follow. But everyone fought about being the fish to see this man. Which is why we were all enemies in the first place. Every time I was in class, I couldn't help but look past where the boats were and feel like I really needed to explore that place. I wanted to, one day, go past those boats and never come back.

Chapter 3

The Fight Within

Ma'an

One day, as I was traveling through Rocky Cove, I saw Badal, one of the oldest Elders in our tribe. I normally tried to avoid the Elders because they always think we youngsters are up to no good. As I swam past him, though, I heard him say to me, "You could be the one!"

Here we go again! I thought. *Another old school zealot!*

Badal spoke up again, "You don't really believe, do you?" I stopped and floated there for a second contemplating what to do. Typically, I would not pay any attention, but I was tired of ignoring the prophecy. I turned and swam back toward him.

As I approached him, I asked, "Have you ever seen the storm get calmed or the ManGod walk on water?"

Badal stared at me in quiet observation and admitted, "No, but I've seen storms."

I looked at him in disbelief. "Are you serious? There have always been storms. Everyone knows this, but what does a storm have to do with a ManGod walking on water?"

Badal again stared at me and said, "Well if the prophecy got the storm part right, then I believe it's just a matter of time before the rest falls into place."

"So, what's stopping it from happening?" I asked, genuinely curious.

He smiled and responded, "If you really want to know, meet me here after school tomorrow and I'll tell you why the prophecy has not come to pass."

I turned around and swam home still thinking about what that old fish said. The next day, after school, I still couldn't shake what the old fish said. I was intrigued. As I swam home, I saw Badal swimming in the same spot I had left him yesterday. He seemed to be in thought. When he looked up and saw me, he got right to the point, "So do you want to know?"

I answered, "Yes."

"Come over to my home and I'll tell you."

I followed Badal to his house. He lived in underwater Rocky Cave that used to be the home of a crab that he fought off. The underwater Rocky Cave was nestled in an overgrown bed of seaweed. As I swam in Badal's home, I found a whole group of Elders floating together in a circle.

He told them, "I have a non-believer."

Great! I thought. *I'm about to get educated by these Elders!*

I was about to swim out when I heard one of them say in a condescending voice, "Your dad believed in our traditions, why don't you?"

I swam around and hovered for a moment or two before looking at them. I said, "I do believe, just not like you all do." An awkward pause followed, and all the Elders just stared at me. Wanting to break the silence, I hastened to continue, "I believe we are all Father Galilee's fishlings."

"Oh, is that so?" asked one of the Elders. "Your father would be ashamed of you! *We* are the descendants of Father Galilee; it is through us that the prophecy will be fulfilled!"

I swam out of there quickly. I couldn't help but think, *What if they are right? What if I am dishonoring my dad's legacy by not believing we are the chosen ones—that it's through us that this prophecy will come to pass?* I swam home and tried not to think about it anymore that night.

The next day after school, I swam into Badal again and he asked me, "Are you going to believe or not? Our traditions teach us that it is from the Sarotherodon that this prophecy will be fulfilled. You know where my house is; you can either float around in life not knowing what your purpose is, or you can truly follow our traditions."

After saying this, Badal swam away. I drifted there and started thinking about when I was a larvae with my dad, and how much I wanted to be the one to fulfill the prophecy. As I thought back to my father and the prophecy, my thoughts turned to my friends. I loved my friends very much, but I knew I couldn't change them anymore than they could change me. I also knew this situation had the potential of dividing our friendship, and I did not want that. I felt confused and sensed a battle raging inside my heart.

At school the following morning, I did not feel like myself. Behind our classes there was a triangular shape that the stone walls of the top of the T shape formed. This was where all the students hung out before school started. I saw a group of Musht fish together. Normally, I'd avoid them because they were traditionalists, but everything Badal discussed with me had me contemplating life and its meaning. I swam to them and said, "Hey!" They all looked astonished as they looked my way because they knew I really didn't care for traditions. I spoke up, not really knowing what to say. I started the conversation with, "So the prophecy..." and I let my voice trail into the water.

"What about it?" One of them asked.

"Well…" I began, and then started to stammer over my words. "Ummm, our family will fulfill it one day!" My voice turned to a falsetto as I continued, "One day." One day! I couldn't believe what had come out of my mouth and how!

I felt embarrassed and started to swim away when I heard one of them speak up and say, "I didn't know you were all about the prophecy."

"Well, you know, I uh…" as I said this it got really quiet and felt like everyone was listening in. I continued, "I do believe in it now and I also believe that we will be the ones to fulfill it."

"I'll dive to that," one of them said. In fish language, that meant "that's lit." I swam away feeling righteous.

Chapter 4

Tsel' the Seer

Tsel'

Another dream. Why do I keep having these dreams and what do they mean? As I slept, I was overwhelmed by a darkness so thick, it felt as if I was suffocating. I was so overcome with this darkness that I felt my body begin to collapse. Fear gripped my soul. Just as I felt myself passing out, I saw a light. This light was unlike any light I had ever seen. It shone so bright that its radiance consumed me. It was like the light was alive. Although it shone on me, I was outside my body looking at my body and behind me there was no shadow. I felt welcomed and loved in this light. It was as if I was home.

During this euphoric moment, I looked to the right and saw the number six facing a mirror. I could not see what was in the mirror. Then I heard a voice—a calming, resounding voice say, "Go see what the reflection of the six is." So, I swam close by it. To my amazement it was not what I thought it would be!

The reflection was a six-letter word. Before I could fully comprehend what I was seeing, the top part of the six fell off, and all that was left was a zero. Its reflection was one letter from the word that was first there, "I."

Immediately that darkness consumed me again and I froze. My body could not move. It was hard for me to speak. I panicked and tried to scream, but no sound was coming out.

Then, I remembered the light. As I reflected on the brilliance of the light, I felt my body come back to life. I woke up shaking uncontrollably. I screamed out, “Mom! Dad!”

My parents came into the room and asked, “What’s the matter?”

“Was it another dream?” My dad asked with a tone of annoyance. I told them yes, and once again told them about my dream. My dad said, “Always remember, dreams are not real...”

Before my dad finished talking, my mom looked at my dad sternly and said, “Pik, they are real to him.” She turned to me and said, “Why don’t you go back to sleep now, Tsel’. You are safe.”

“But I saw a light!” I spoke up in desperation. My dad had already headed back to his room, but my mom looked at me as if she was contemplating something weighty. “What is it mom?”

“Nothing sweetheart. Go back to bed. You have school tomorrow.”

As I laid back down, I couldn’t help but wonder why my mom looked at me that way.

I listened closely—maybe I could overhear my mom and dad talking. There was complete silence, so I got up and silently swam by their room. All I heard was my mom say, “You think he has my mother’s gift of seeing?”

My dad responded, “Your mom was crazy.”

I swam back to my room to think over what they said, but fell asleep. The next thing I knew, I was waking to another day.

Chapter 5

Our Reflection

Ma'an

"Where are you going?" my mom called after me.

"Just for a fast swim, Mom!"

"Alright Ma'an, but I want you back in 30 minutes. Our shoal found a good place to eat; there is some delicious food on the ground about 500 fins west of our home."

"Okay!"

It was time to meet up with the crew and I was anxious to see them. I went to our boat club. I looked around and no one was there. I heard a noise to the left of me and froze. "Who is there!?" There was no answer.

With my left eye I could see what looked like two whiskers floating on the sides of something. My heart stopped, it...it...it's... I took my fins and covered my eyes. I remembered that I barely escaped last time. This time there was no way I was getting away.

Then I heard a deep laugh and I realized who it was. "Guys, that's not funny!" I said, in a bit of a put-out tone.

Alziwaq smoothly said, "Got you!"

Tsel' chimed in with his deep voice, "We got you!"

"Whatever!" I said irritatingly. "I knew it was you guys all along."

"Sure," they said. Tsel' had this look on his face as if he had done something wrong. Alziwaq and I looked at each other, we were on the verge of asking him why he appeared guilty when we heard some giggling.

We turned around and saw three girls swimming toward our boat club. Each girl was from one of our families. From my family was Mar'ah[viii], she was in the Simonis clan. She was very shy, a perfectionist, and wise. Unlike my blue coloration and multicolored scales, her clan was a wide variety of shimmering purple.

From the Cyprinidae family was Aineakas (Ah-nah-Kay-Sa). Unlike Alziwaq, Aineakas was in the Canis clan. She was loud and always had something to say. She never backed down from a challenge.

Lastly, from Tsel's clan, was Zerkalo (Zēr-ka-la)[ix] who was very discerning and mysterious.

Aineakas was the first one to break the silence and asked, "What are you boys doing this far from home? Don't you know you're not supposed to be out here?"

"Yeah!" exclaimed Mar'ah, and Zerkalo nodded her head in agreement.

Just when I was about to speak, Aineakas admitted, "I'm just joking! Relax."

Alziwaq and I looked at Tsel' and he said, "What? They pressured me and... and... well, they're here now. Let's just deal with it."

I looked at the girls and said, "You are not welcome here." Alziwaq nodded in agreement.

Aineakas swam close to me, pointed her fin at me, and said, "When you're in trouble and you begin to reflect, remember you thought you did not need us! Come on ladies, let's go!"

Tsel' begged, "Wait, come back!" The girls paid no attention and kept swimming until we couldn't see them anymore.

Tsel' looked at us until Alziwaq said, "I could eat you!"

Tsel' responded, "I bet you would, you fat whale!"

"What did you call me?" Alziwaq shot back.

I could sense the tension rising between them, so I jumped between them. "Fish! Fish! Calm down!"

Tsel' proclaimed, "I'm out of here!"

Alziwaq huffed, "Fine! Leave!"

Tsel' looked at me with disdain and swam back home. I looked at Alziwaq and was about to say something, but remembered I had to be back home for dinner. I quickly said, "I have to go. I just remembered I promised my mom I'd be back for dinner." I started to swim off, then quickly circled back around and added, "I'm sure everything will be back to normal between you and Tsel' soon." I raced back toward home as soon as I could. I decided to go where my mom said they would be. As I swam closer, I could see they had almost cleared out everything from the ground.

My mom saw me and said, "So nice of you to join us! You have got to be careful hanging out with those boys."

I looked at her shocked. She knew of me and my friends? I quickly asked, "What boys?"

"I'm not dumb!" My mother answered. "I've been around longer than you! Just be careful." She continued to graze the food from the bottom.

Chapter 6

Supernatural Knowledge

Alziwaq

Ever since I can remember, I have always had insight about things that I have never been told. The way I see it, some of these things I have no business knowing (such as trouble in families), and some things, maybe I should know more of (like an instinct with how there are different planets in the sky above before we even learned it in school). Sometimes, when I'm around other fish—whether I know them or not—I get an inclination about what happened in their life or what is currently happening in their life. It was as if someone opened up a book of their life to me and I could see their past and present.

Learning about our minds and how to distinguish between insight and opinions was not something taught in our world, specifically with the Biny clan. We were taught survival. Our lives were all about the survival of the fish; either you were the strongest, or the weakest of the clan, there was no room for in-between. We never discussed when there was a disagreement within our group, we fought to get the resolution at all costs, even if it meant death. In other words, you didn't want to be a fish caught in the wrong neighborhood. If you happened to find yourself in this predicament, chances are, you wouldn't survive the night.

Both my parents died when I was little, so I grew up with my Uncle Qua. Being brought up in ancient rules and ways meant if you were not on his side then you were just in the way.

One day, as I was making my way home from one of our assembles, I was hoping my uncle wouldn't be home. Even though I was grateful he took me in after I lost my parents, I was afraid of him because he would yell at me for things I did that he thought were wrong, even if I wasn't being purposely disobedient. Upon entering the house, I suddenly felt a force hit my stomach. It knocked the water out of me.

"Hey nerd!" my uncle greeted.

"Hey Unc," I responded sheepishly. Without warning, it happened. I had a Word of Knowledge. I knew my uncle had done something wrong. I looked at him with an intense look.

He asked, "Why are you looking at me like that?"

"Because I know exactly what you did."

"I didn't do anything boy!" he argued aggressively.

"Yes, you did! You and your buddies caught one of them!" He was shocked that I knew.

"How did you…? Never mind! You stay outta my business! We're gonna teach him a thing or two about killing our clan! We're tying him up to a wood board. You should come watch how real men handle things!"

I couldn't believe what I was hearing. I looked at him and said, "It's against fish code! We don't believe in vengeance anymore, ever since the *Fish Wars* between the families!"

This made him angry and he swam quickly toward me. I thought he was going to hit me, but he simply said, "You coward. Get out of my house!" I was accustomed to him throwing temper tantrums; I knew it was no use arguing with him, so I swam out.

As I was leaving, I looked to the left side of the home and I saw a small, helpless fish tied up in a fish net. At first glance, my thought was, *that's not my problem*, but I felt I needed to set it free before I left. I looked around and I could see my uncle greeting his friends who had just arrived at the house. I knew as they went into

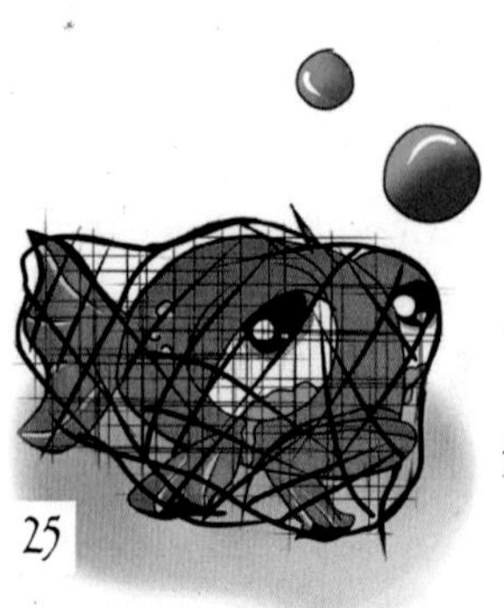

the house, they were going to eat some snails and plan the execution of the fish they caught. If I was going to free him, now would be the time. I quickly rushed toward the fish. As I came closer, it became more apparent to me they had caught a fingerling.

They had wrapped him in pieces of nets that humans used to catch us. I quickly looked around for something sharp because I could not tear into the pieces of net with my teeth. I caught a glimpse of something silver reflecting from the ground with a pointy end. I swam to it and saw that it was a broken piece from one of the things that hold the ships together. I carefully picked it up with my mouth making sure I did not cut my mouth and began to cut the net with the sharp edges until I freed him.

When he was free, the fish just looked at me stunned. We just stared at each other for what seemed like an eternity. Then he said, "You'll all pay!" and swam off quickly, the murky water dissolving his presence. I stood there silently thinking, *What a salty fish! He didn't even say thank you!* In the distance I could overhear my uncle saying, "I can't wait to take care of that fish!" I knew I had to quickly leave. If he found out it was me who freed the fish, that would be the end—you never betray your own. I quickly took off for our clubhouse, not knowing if I'd be able to go back home again.

Chapter 7

There's an 'I' in Right

Ma'an

The next day I headed to our usual hangout. Upon my arrival, I was both shocked and happy to see Alziwaq and Tsel' waiting for me. I looked at both of them and asked, "What's up?"

"We need to talk," they both said in unison, their tones reluctant.

"What is it we need to talk about?" I asked inquisitively.

"Well, one fish told us that you believe your family was destined to find the coin," Tsel' said.

I laughed nervously, then looked at both of them and inquired, "Really guys. Does this even matter?"

Alziwaq's voice was filled with concern and he asked smoothly, "Is it true?"

Tsel' looked at me, waiting with anticipation. I looked at them and answered, "Yes, but it's only because our clan was the first to hear of the prophecy." They just shook their heads at me in disgust. In that very moment, I felt indignation well up inside me. I knew it was ugly, but I did not care. "I'm so sorry that my beliefs offend you! It's not like I lied though. What I said was right."

Tsel' responded, "I thought you were different from the others, but I realize you have just as much pride as they do."

I looked at them and defended myself, "Don't talk to me about pride! Look at you guys! You each still have both your parents, all I have is my mom."

Tsel' looked at me with disbelief and solemnly responded, "Alziwaq lost both of his parents, remember?"

I realized, then, I was hurting my friends. But my desire to be right outweighed my love for them. I looked at them and proclaimed, "I'm not going to be sorry for telling the truth. My family is rightfully chosen. This is our destiny; I will find that coin."

"Maybe you will, but it will be without me!" Tsel' exclaimed. "I'm out of here, and if we ever cross water again, don't act like you know me." With that, he turned and swam away.

Alziwaq looked at me and said, "Someone once told me that love is not self-seeking, it doesn't care about being right in its own eyes. It cares more about being right with others through forgiveness and patience. This does not mean it longs to please others. Another fish's approval should never dictate your life. What it means instead, is that I would rather be offended than carry offense."

What Alziwaq said was powerful to listen to, but for some reason it did nothing to change my heart. My mind was set. What the Elders spoke to me was all I could reason with. Our traditions, for me, were the only thing that still connected me to my dad. Abandoning them, I realized, would be like killing him again.

Chapter 8

Ma'an meets with Professor Mo

Ma'an

After our fight, Tsel', Alziwaq, and I hardly spoke to each other at school anymore and I didn't go back to the clubhouse. I thought, *I don't need them.* As I sat in Professor MoAwesome's class, my mind was somewhere else, out past the shipwrecks. I was determined to talk to Professor Mo after school to discuss what was on my mind.

As soon as we were released from class, I stayed in my seat and waited until all the fish left. Then I approached him. I nervously asked, "Hi...Professor MoAwesome, umm... can I ask something?" I'd never gotten this close to him before. I could see some scars on his right side, and I couldn't help but stare at them.

He looked at me and asked, "Is it about my scars?"

Feeling embarrassed, I quickly said, "No! . . . Uh, sorry. It's about the prophecy."

"What about it?" He sounded irritated.

"Well, I heard you knew more about the prophecy?" I added quickly.

"Aren't you afraid of me, like the other fingerlings?" I just stared at him. "Don't you know I could. . ." He paused and then launched at me, laughing, saying, "EAT YOU?!"

I did not know what to make of this, but I did not feel in any danger. Right then, there was a noise. I turned to look at where it came from. When I looked back, I saw Professor Mo under the stony table, shaking.

At that moment, I realized that all the stuff the fish had said about him were all false. He was (in fish language) what we call, *bubble*. Bubble meant someone who could easily pop under pressure. I looked at him and asked, "Is everything okay?"

Welcome
-b ± √b² - 4ac
2a
BETA
BETA
BETA

He quickly jumped up, “Yes, everything is good. Why wouldn’t it be?” Then he quickly changed the subject back to the prophecy.

“Well you’re not who I thought you were,” I said.

MoAwesome looked at me with disbelief, “Why? Is it because you realized I, too, have weaknesses?” I averted my eyes and remained silent. He continued, “Listen, fingerling, life is not about how strong a fish is, it’s about admitting when you need help and trusting in something greater than yourself.”

I stopped, and although I could not fully grasp what he was saying, I looked at him and said, “I’m listening.”

He then began to tell me there was more to the prophecy than what meets the eye. He talked about when he was young, his father told him a story that his father told him, “My grandfather was just a larvae on the day he swam up toward the surface one evening in the spring.” As MoAwesome told the story to me, he became animated, and he held a far-off gaze in his eye. As if remembering where he was, he paused and studied me for a moment before continuing, “Upon reaching the surface, there it was!” MoAwesome spoke the last words in a whisper.

“There what was?” I asked immediately.

“The Light,” responded MoAwesome. I nodded for him to go on and MoAwesome continued to tell me about the light he saw. He described it as a light from the sky that beamed down over a particular place. “This light was unlike any light he had ever seen—it did not move! It was like. . .”

“It was like what?” I asked anxiously.

“It was like a sign that the prophecy had started. From that day on my grandfather, my father, and now I had not stopped going to the surface, whenever there is a storm, in hopes we could still see the prophecy fulfilled.” After telling me this, he looked at me and said, "I've always thought it would be someone from our clan that would fulfill the prophecy but I was wrong. I now know it's going to take all of us working together to fulfill it because we are all Father Galilee's offspring, whether it's by birth or by belief."

I couldn't believe what I heard! MoAwesome said what I used to believe!

As I floated there staring at him, he looked at me and said, "There are these ladies who live in the center of the Sea. They are the Seers. They serve the One who is called AGAPE whose spirit is very mansuetude. No one is meeker than He is, and He is ardently truthful. But you cannot do this by yourself; they will only speak to the one who sees the storm calmed and the ManGod walking on water. To find them—if you were the one—follow the sun backward until you reach the deep springs of the abyss. There will be six underwater springs in a circle and the seventh will be in the middle of them all. In one of these springs they abide."

Chapter 9

Paragon

Ma'an

There was a lot to think about after I left MoAwesome. I swam home not knowing how to feel. When I got home my mom called my name.

"Yes, Mom?" I responded.

She went on to say, "Come here. I want to talk to you about our last conversation."

"Not again!" I sighed under my breath. "I already listened to you and got rid of those friends." She looked at me unhappily. I said, "You told me to be careful. . ."

Before I finished, she swam next to me, embraced me and said, "Ma'an, I did not say what I said because they were from different families, I just wanted you to be cautious."

I stared at her, feeling very numb. "Can I go to bed now? It's kind of late."

"Sure."

I swam down to my room. I was angry, so angry! *How could they be so mean to me like they were. I'll show them! I thought to myself. Every day I'm going to swim up to the surface until I fulfill the prophecy.*

As I slept that night, I felt heavy. There was a subtle, beautiful melody that started to play in my mind. I was taken aback by the sound; I could not figure out where this symphony-like music was coming from. Right when it seemed to end, there was a modulation cadence, another musical note was played. Then suddenly the musical euphony stopped. After the combination of tone and rhythm ceased, I heard the name

"Paragon" whispered in my room. I said, "Who's there?" Dead silence was the only response and I thought, *I must be losing my mind.*

Suddenly, I heard a voice that spoke cunningly, "I'm Paragon. I am whoever you want me to be." I looked into my dark room and saw what seemed like shiny stones shimmering.

"Wha—what do you want?" I stammered.

He responded, "It's not what I want, but what you want, more than anything."

I felt this declaration pull inside me and I said, "You have my attention."

The voice spoke back, "Give in to your hate; use it as something that will drive you. Allow it to guide you. Don't forgive. . . do all this and you will achieve what you're looking for."

I did not say anything back; I thought, *How did it know that I wanted to fulfill the prophecy?*

Paragon continued and said, "I know how you can fulfill the prophecy. There is a temple to the south of the Sea. Go there and I will give you the coin."

The next day I went to Professor Mo and asked him, "Is there a temple to the south of us?"

Looking at me sternly MoAwesome asked, "Who told you about the Temple?"

"I overheard someone talking about it, that's all."

"Look at these scars!" MoAwesome spoke in a tone I had never heard from him before. "Let the scars be a warning to you! Do not go to the Temple!"

Leaving his class, I could feel the anger rising inside of me, and these thoughts came into my mind, *MoAwesome must be withholding something from me! Why else would he have kept the information about the Temple from me when we were first talking?* I remembered that to go south I just had to watch where the sun rises and where it sets. I remembered the sun rises in the east and sets in the west. I also knew that the current flows to the south, but it was also hard to truly find the current. I still had to figure out how to differentiate between north and south.

I knew I had to leave early in the morning, before my mom woke up. So, before the sun came up, I snuck out, swam up to the surface, and waited for the sun to rise. As it rose, I swam down to the bottom of the sea and began using stones to map out the sun. I did this in order to find out its exact path. Every three hours, I would go up and see the sun's course. Then I would come down and place another stone until the sun set. By the end of the day, I knew which way was east and which way was west. I still struggled with figuring out which way was north and south. I was determined to find out sometime tomorrow.

The next day in school, one of my professors—who taught us how to find our way when lost—talked about a light that shines the brightest in the night. He said it's not the *biggest* light but it's the *brightest*. As the night came, I wasted no time swimming up to the surface. Once I reached it, I looked up at the sky and saw the *Light*. This was my last marker; I had what I needed to go to the Temple.

Chapter 10

The Storm is Calmed

Ma'an

The morning came and I set out without telling anyone I was leaving, let alone where I was going. I knew if they found out they would try to stop me, and I was determined to fulfill my mission to see the Temple. I began to swim and when I got to our clubhouse, I stopped for a moment. For the first time in my life I went passed the shipwreck. As I was swimming, I thought I heard someone call my name. I stopped for a second, then I heard a voice say, "Don't look back." I kept pressing forward, toward a place I had never been, excited and scared at the same time. Without warning, something transpired that I did not intend to happen. As I looked up, I saw a multitude of lightning and heard rumblings of thunder. What had been a calm day only moments before, had turned into a dark night. I was being tossed back and forth violently; I had never been in a storm like this before. There was also an internal battle inside me.

I could hear what seemed like a peaceful voice say to me, "Go and see." No sooner were those words spoken, I heard another voice say, "You already have the coin." I waited for what seemed like forever. Then I jolted up swimming frantically toward the surface. What I witnessed could only be described as a dream.

Coming out of the water, I saw what looked like 30,000 fins-high waves coming straight toward me. In the midst of all the waves, there it was: a boat. As I turned to swim back, I could hear the men screaming, "Help! We're sinking!" Just as I thought, *Another foolish boat that's going to be a part of the clubhouse,* I heard one of them say, "Wake up the Master!"

I turned back around and saw a man come up from the bottom of the boat. He stared at the sea and the storm and simply demanded, "Peace Be Still!" The waves all flattened, the clouds all rolled back, much like the front of seaweed unfurls. The sun shone bright and the bluest sky I had ever seen appeared.

I couldn't believe what I was watching. It was Him! He really was here! The man didn't shine like I thought he would. He looked like a common man, but spoke like he was the Creator of the Sea. I heard him say to the men with him, "Why are you so afraid? Have you still no faith?"

I floated there in amazement and watched as the boat went on to the other side. I swam back down and could not believe what I had just witnessed. I wanted to go tell the others but I couldn't seem to gather the courage to.

The words the man spoke were continuously ringing in my otoliths, "*Why are you so afraid? Have you still no faith?*" I couldn't help but wonder if I still had faith. I felt confused. Paragon had promised me the Coin, but I just saw the first of the prophecy. Then again, if it was not for Paragon telling me to go to the Temple, I most certainly would have never seen the ManGod calming the storm. I floated there, lost in my thoughts and uncertain of what to do next. Then a thought came to me, *What about the Seers?* There was so much confusion in my mind that this thought was relieving. Knowing what I was doing next brought peace to my heart. I headed toward the center of the Sea where the Seers lived.

Chapter 11

Where is Ma'an?

The Narrator

"Has anyone seen my son? Someone, help!" Ma'an's mother swam around frantically screaming.

"What is it Ms. Penayel?" asked Mr. Gayvaw, the director of the schools.

"It's my son," Penayel cried. "I have not seen him for the last two days!"

"Have you checked with your clan? We all know that his father loved to..." Mr. Gayvaw paused when he realized that Penayel was not in a good mood. "I'll tell you what," said Mr. Gayvaw. "I'll let all the professors know about your son, Ma'an, and they can ask the other fishlings if they have seen him. But there is a good chance... well yeah."

The director made an announcement through the snail shell that helped his voice carry throughout the school. Tsel' and Alziwaq exchanged disturbed glances with one another when they heard it. They abruptly left their classroom and quickly swam out. They headed to Ms. Penayel's place. For the first time in generations, two fish from other tribes came to the Musht tribe's home without the Elders' approval. It was not a welcoming moment. Many of the Elder fish angrily approached and threatened them.

This did not deter them though. They boldly said, "We need to speak to Ms. Penayel. We think we know which way Ma'an may have gone."

At that moment, Ms. Penayel came out and told the crowd that had gathered around them, in an angry tone, "The last thing you want to do, is mess with me right now, you fish better leave these fingerlings alone!" After hearing her speak, each of them reluctantly went back to their Rocky Cove. "Boys, come into my house and tell me where you think Ma'an is," she said with a sad look on her face.

They went into her home and Alziwaq spoke up, "I saw him two days ago headed beyond the shipwreck."

Ms. Penayel sighed and shook her head as if what Alziwaq said confirmed what she already felt in her heart. She looked at them for a long time and asked, "What are you guys going to do about it?"

Not expecting this response, they halted, not knowing what to say back to her.

Ms. Penayel continued, "My son loves you guys. I know there was a fall out between you three, but always remember the word *friend* has the word *end* in it. Not because it's meant to end, but because it endures 'til the end. Now I'm old, I cannot go after my son, but. . ."

Before she finished her sentence, Tsel' spoke up, "We know what we have to do."

They headed out of the house and back to the school. "There's only one fish who can help us now," said Alziwaq.

Tsel' responded emphatically, "Professor Mo."

By the time they arrived, school was over and they rushed to Professor Mo. "Professor! Professor!" they shouted.

"What is it now!?" MoAwesome asked sternly.

Tsel' and Alziwaq looked at each other and Tsel' said in his deep voice, "Ma'an is missing and we thought, well we know that you know the Sea better than anyone else. . ." Tsel's voice trailed off.

Alziwaq chimed in, "Could you help us find him?"

MoAwesome looked at them intensely and asked, "Why are you both together?"

Tsel' and Alziwaq were taken aback by the question. He pressed, "Well?

Alziwaq spoke up in his smooth voice, "No matter what scales a fish has, he's still a fish and that's all that matters to us."

MoAwesome smiled and simply said, "Good."

He then began to tell them all he told Ma'an, but then he stopped. They both asked, "What is it?"

He looked at them and answered, "He brought up the Temple."

"What is that?" Tsel' asked.

"It's a place of pain. I once was drawn there by the one they call Paragon. If Ma'an is headed there, indeed, we may never see him again."

"How did you escape?" asked Tsel'.

"Escape? Who said I escaped?" MoAwesome's tone slightly scoffed at the memory, then softened when he continued, "I was saved by Agape, the Magnanimous One."

"Who is He and how do we find Him?" they both asked.

MoAwesome looked into their eyes and answered, "If you seek Him ardently, you'll find Him. Now listen closely, there are these Seers who live in the center of the Sea. Although they will only speak to you if you have fulfilled the prophecy, maybe, just maybe, they will know more. Follow the sun backward until you reach six springs in a circle with the seventh in the middle; in one of these springs they abide."

Chapter 12

Ma'an and the Seers

Ma'an

I found some rocks stacked with cave-like holes between them where I could sleep in for the night. When morning came, I pondered what Professor Mo told me: "Follow the sun backward." What did it mean to follow the sun backward? Just then I heard some humming. "Who's there?" I asked.

The humming grew louder and louder as whatever this mysterious creature was got closer. When I saw it, I exhaled water in relief. It was a Salaria fish. Salaria fish were not big and had a very defined face. They remained nameless; it was for their protection. He looked at me and asked mischievously, "How can I be of service?" I was always told they were the most helpful kind of fish in the Sea, but it was not free.

I pondered whether or not to get tangled up with this Salaria. I looked at him and decided to engage, "I'm puzzled by something my Professor told me."

"Puzzle? I love Puzzles! Tell me," he said deviously.

I asked him, "What will I owe you if you solve it for me?"

He grinned and answered, "What I need most."

"What's that?" I asked irritatingly.

"I mustn't tell unless you say no. So, if you want my help, I will help and if I help, you will owe," he replied. I agreed. I told him what my professor said, and he floated backward a bit and exclaimed, "A difficult puzzle indeed!"

I stared at him and desperately asked, "Do you know what it means?"

He replied, "Of course, I do." But he just floated there. It made me a little bit mad and he could tell I was getting angry. He told me, "You should really control your temper."

I quickly added, "I did not ask you to be my counselor. Are you going to tell me or not? If you're not, I'm out of here!" As I started to swim away, he said, "Where the sun rises, it does not set. Where the sun sets, it does not rise."

What in the world did that mean? I looked at him and said, "So I ask you for help to solve something that was hard to understand and you tell me something that's even harder to comprehend! I'm going to. . ." As I was speaking, I thought about what he said, and it actually made sense. The sun only rises in the east and sets in the west, so I need to go east when it's rising. I must follow the sun backward. "Okay, what do you need me to do?" I asked.

Looking at me, he said, "I need you to stop being so angry."

I was thrown off by what he said. Frustrated, I swam away toward the sunrise. The nerves that fish had, I thought.

I swam for what seemed like four hours and found some food on the bottom of the sea. After eating, I continued through the water not sure what to expect. My surroundings were unlike anything I had ever seen. There were so many different fish swimming and living life. The underwater mountains were covered in algae and little animals called zooplankton that glowed majestically. It was awe inspiring, but I did not have time to take it in. There was a path between the mountains that I followed, rushing by all the fish in a hurry to get where I wanted to go. I swam on until I saw the dark abyss. It looked deep and scary, but I was not going to turn back now.

I swam down deeper until I saw the six springs in a circle with the seventh in the middle. I was bewildered by what I was seeing. The middle spring was red and all the other ones were white. As I came closer, I heard a voice ask, "Why do you come to us?"

With terror in my voice I answered, "I am here because I have fulfilled the prophecy!"

"Are you alone?"

"Yes," I replied.

"Then you lie! The journey was not meant to be done by one alone, but those who are one. In addition, Agape tells us there is unforgiveness in your heart. You are, at this moment, not the one. Before you leave, remember that purpose must be spoken in three different ways by whom purpose belongs to and it must be reflected three different ways each time by they who are reflection by name."

"What do you mean by that?" When they didn't respond right away, I became angry and yelled, "I don't need you! I'll do it myself!" I couldn't believe what they said and that they refused to answer me! I'd come too far to stop now! "Paragon is the only one who is for me! What he says is easy to understand! I'm heading to the Temple!"

Chapter 13

Tsel' and Alziwaq go meet the Seers

The Narrator

"What do we do?" Alziwaq asked Tsel'.

Tsel' answered, "We must go meet with the Seers,"

"But you heard professor Mo," Alziwaq said. "They will only speak to us if we fulfilled two parts of the prophecy: seeing the storm calmed and the ManGod walking on water."

"Maybe they know where Ma'an is, and that's worth trying. Let's meet up at the clubhouse in about two hours. I have to let my mom know, but I know my dad won't understand," said Tsel'.

"Mom!" Tsel' called out when he got home.

"What is it?" she answered.

"You know that boy that got lost?"

"From the Mu family?"

"Yes."

"What about him?" she asked.

"I may know where he is and Alziwaq and I—,"

"WAIT, WHO'S ALZIWAQ? YOU'RE NOT HANGING OUT WITH THE OTHER FAMILIES ARE YOU!?!" she yelled.

"Yes, but I can explain," Tsel' started quietly.

Just then, Tsel's dad came in and asked, "What's with all the commotion?"

"Your son is hanging out with the other families!" Tsel's mother explained.

"You're grounded!" Tsel's dad yelled back without needing an explanation.

"Mom, Dad he could be in trouble!" Tsel' exclaimed in a panicked tone.

His mom began to calm down and looked at his dad, who said, "Don't you give in, Vyslushat."

She responded, "If his friend is in trouble, shouldn't we help?" She looked at Tsel' and continued, "The dream you had means a lot more than you know. My mother used to dream as you do, until one day she dreamt that someone named Agape was calling her to go. She listened and left. When my mother dreamed something, it almost always happened as she saw it. She felt her purpose was to obey and go. I trust you feel your purpose is to save your friend?"

"I do, Mom," Tsel' answered quietly.

"Honey," she looked at my dad. "We must let him go."

Pik looked unsure. After about a minute of thinking he spoke up, "I'm not on board with this decision." Hearing this, Tsel's face became sad. Continuing on, his dad said, "but I know what it's like to lose a friend." In saying this Tsel' and his mom knew that he was talking about his best friend. Tsel's dad blamed himself for not rescuing him when he had been caught in a net years ago.

Tsel' and his mom looked at Pik and Tsel' said, "Dad you cannot guilt yourself over the past."

Pik looked back at Tsel' and replied, "You're right and I also do believe you should go rescue your friend." Tsel' hugged and kissed both of them and swam toward the boat club.

"Be careful!" His mom hollered.

"I will!" Tsel' yelled back. As he arrived at the boat, he saw Alziwaq waiting for him. "Let's go," Tsel' said.

Alziwaq looked at him and said, "What direction do we go?"

"We must 'follow the sun backward.'" They both contemplated what that meant.

Alziwaq spoke up, "Should we ask a Salaria?"

Tsel' quickly replied, "NO!"

"Okay, okay! Why not?" Alziwaq inquired.

Tsel' didn't even look at Alziwaq. It was as if he was lost in his own mind. He suddenly said, still not looking at him, "I cannot talk about it right now; let's just say they made me do something that no fish should ever do."

Just then, it dawned on Tsel', "What if we ask, Mar'ah? I know what you're thinking, but she is very wise."

Alziwaq sat there quietly and then admitted, "We can use all the help we can get."

They both went to the school and saw her in class. The teacher was lecturing. "How can we get her attention?" they both silently mouthed.

Alziwaq thought of a brilliant idea, "How about I distract the professor, while you sneak in there and speak to her?" Alziwaq went toward the professor and said, "My stomach hurts; I may have eaten too many snails."

The professor was caught off guard and did not know what to say so he just stared at him. Alziwaq held his water and began to float up toward the surface. The professor, who was from the Kinneret family, frantically tried to get him down, but Alziwaq weighed so much that it was nearly impossible. The whole class was laughing. Tsel' snuck into where Mar'ah was and when she saw him, she said, "Great! What do you want?"

"We need your help," Tsel' whispered to her.

"You should have thought about that before you kicked me out of your club!"

"But that wasn't me. We are sorry!" Tsel' responded.

"What about Ma'an? Is he sorry, too?" she asked with attitude.

"Yeah, about him. . . that's why we're here. Ma'an is lost and we think we may know how to help him."

"I'm listening," said Mar'ah.

"Okay, so how does one go about following the sun backward?"

"Head toward the place where the sun started, silly!"

Tsel' looked embarrassed. "Oh yeah, we knew that," he laughed.

"Where are you guys going?"

"We're headed to the Seers; they may be able to help us find Ma'an. We were told we needed to follow the sun backward. I mean he could have just said east to begin with. Man, that professor! Anyway, we're supposed to go 'til we reach six springs and the seventh one will be in the middle." Mar'ah was silent, she just sat there thinking. Tsel', seeing the professor coming back down because Alziwaq couldn't hold his water anymore, said, "Thanks Mar'ah." He swam off toward Alziwaq.

As soon as Alziwaq saw Tsel' leave he said, "Wow, I feel so much better, thanks! Bye!" And with that, they swam off.

"You boys think this is a joke?!" The professor yelled at them as the class roared in laughter.

The boys headed east until they got to the Underwater Mountains. The mountains were covered in little tiny animals called Zooplankton. The chemicals in these animals caused a light to shine from them called luciferins. There were so many Zooplanktons on these mountains that they were glowing. It was a site to behold! Parts of the mountains had algae which attracted micro animals called Phytoplankton. Phytoplankton were the food source of the Zooplanktons[x]. Alziwaq quickly snatched a snail from the mountain. There were so many different species of fish that it was almost overwhelming for Alziwaq and Tsel'. The mountains were on either side of them and there was almost a path right down the middle. It was hard for them to even number all the mountains. All the fish swam down the middle going about their day. It was a fish highway. Tsel' stopped swimming and just floated there. He looked at Alziwaq and said, "Let's take it all in. My mother once told me that those who live a life of awe and wonder truly live."

After a minute, Alziwaq jokingly said, "That's pretty deep." Realizing, though, that Tsel' was pretty serious, Alziwaq cleared his gills and said, "I'll dive to that." As they neared the end of this water highway, they saw a dark abyss and reluctantly headed down into it. It was dark as they went in, but they kept going. There was, in front of them, six springs that shone white and, in the middle, there was a seventh red spring.

Getting closer, they heard two voices speak in unison, "Why are you here?"

"We are looking for a friend," the boys said full of fear.

"Your friend is not here, but you have a dream to tell us."

Alziwaq looked confused, and Tsel' spoke up and asked, "How did you know I had a dream to tell you?" Suddenly, two lady fish came out from the white spring in front of them. They were old, yet stunning, their faces shone. They had long eyelashes and their eyes were fierce.

One of them was from Tsel's tribe; she looked at him and smiled. He didn't know what to say but she said, “I know you had a dream because I also dream like you.”

Tsel’ was taken aback and realized, “Grandma Mae!”

“Yes, sweetie?” He quickly swam toward her and embraced her. “Who is your friend?” she asked.

Tsel’ said, “This is Alziwaq.”

“Good to meet you Alziwaq. My name is Mae and this is my friend Lynn.” Lynn was from the Biny family like Alziwaq and she looked at him as if she was about to say something when Grandma Mae said in a peaceful voice, “Tell me your dream Tsel’.”

Tsel’ started to tell his dream, “As I slept, I was overwhelmed by darkness that was so thick it felt as if I was suffocating. As soon as I thought I was going to pass out, a light shone. This light was unlike any light I had ever seen. It consumed me. It was like the light was alive. Although it shone on me, behind me there was no shadow. I felt welcomed and loved—as if I was home. During this euphoric moment, I looked to the right of me and I saw the number six facing a mirror. But I could not see what was in the mirror. I heard a voice, a calming resounding voice, say, ‘Go see what the reflection of the six is.’ So, I swam close by it. To my amazement, it was not what I thought it would be. The reflection was a six-letter word. Before I could fully comprehend what I was seeing, the top part of the six fell off and all that was left was a zero, and its reflection was one letter from the word that was first there, ‘*I*.’”

Lynn spoke up and asked, “Was the word you saw *united*?”

Tsel’ was shocked and swam back. “Yes... How did you...”

Before he finished talking, his grandmother replied, "All we know is not our own, it wasn't earned, it was taught to us by Him to whom we belong. Your dream is depicting your purpose. You are one of the six." She looked at Alziwaq, "You too are one of the six; four of you are missing. There is a saying, 'purpose must be spoken in three different ways by whom purpose belongs to, and it must be reflected three different ways each time by they who are reflection by name.'" Mae looked at her confused grandson. "This, I cannot tell you, but you know." Tsel' floated there troubled, and his grandmother asked, "Do you know what your name means?"

"No," said Tsel'. "What does it mean?"

"Purpose. Now go, find your friend. He headed to the Temple. Follow the current south until you reach the site; don't give up. Be discreet about your plans, for the One Who Reflects Light but Has None of His Own has little creatures that do his bidding. Also, there are three girls who are close behind you; take them with you."

Chapter 14

Mar'ah the Wise

Mar'ah

From the moment of my birth, I was uncommonly quiet. My mom told me that I wouldn't cry or scream as other fish do. As I grew up, I remained demure. Part of that was personality, part of it was the fact that my brother, David, did all the talking on my behalf. I'd rather observe what everyone else was doing than talk anyway. There was much to learn by watching fish. One thing was that all fish had innate evil tendencies. *Every fish for themselves!* It was impossible to find anything or anyone trustworthy. So, I avoid big pools of fish.

I heard the prophecy, but I tried to rationalize it. You couldn't just believe everything someone told you, unless you want to be a snail—which is a very insulting term, by the way. Calling someone a snail is saying they are gullible, ignorant, and slow! I'm a lot like my father, Melech, even though he didn't see it at first. We both loved to just observe people and we always felt that we could do things better than most fish. My mother, Milcah, was the complete opposite, but this was a blessing, it helped me with my perfectionist ways. When you're a perfectionist you tend to think that your way is the best way, so when my mom would do things her way and they would work it was humbling.

They both taught us about Agape. He was the originator of the prophecy. I remember asking them if Agape was fair. Not all fish were the same and it bothered me that there seemed to be a hierarchy with all the fish. My mom just said, "No," and left it at that.

Seeing my confusion, my dad expounded on my mother's answer, "If Agape was fair, Mar'ah, all fish would be dead. You see, Agape knows the heart and the motives of fish." My father stared intently at me as he said this last part. "We all have bad motives that we sometimes act on. If He judged us on fairness, we all would be punished."

After they said this I asked, "So, why are we still here?"

My mother, who was full of compassion, said, "Mercy triumphs over judgement and Agape is full of mercy."

I remembered my parents' words after Tsel' left the class and headed out to find Ma'an. At first, I thought he deserved whatever was coming to him, but as I reflected on my life and all that my mother and father taught me about Agape, I knew it was incumbent of me to help.

Plus, those boys couldn't make it a day without us girls.

It was in that moment of realization about Agape's mercy that I tried to get ahold of my friend Aineakas, who was arguing with the professor about her assignment. She finally swam back to her rocky chair that was next to me. I looked at her and she could pretty much read my mind. Aineakas, Zerkalo, and I had been friends for so long! They saved my life once. I remember it like it was yesterday.

We were all playing by some stones, there was a cave right next to them. Some of the Biny fish waited 'til I was swimming next to the cave and two of them pushed me in, while the others pushed the rock that was on top of the cave down so that the entrance was shut. I panicked! There was no way out for me! There were some holes, but they were too small for me! I didn't know what to do or what was to become of me! I had yet to meet Zerkalo and Aineakas. In fact, I couldn't say I had any real friends to call at this point in time. It was in this moment of despair that Zerkalo swam into the cave through one of the small holes. She looked at me and said, "Hi, I'm Zerkalo! Don't worry! We'll find a way to get out!" It was so comforting knowing that someone had seen what had happened to me and that I was not alone.

I could hear commotion outside the cave. "I'll be right back. Hold on," Zerkalo said, and she swam out the top hole.

Outside the cave, a girl by the name of Aineakas was yelling at the boys who were from her own tribe. She yelled, "If you guys don't help me get her out, so help me!"

One of the fish that pushed me in said, "Why should we help her? She is an infidel—she is not part of our clan."

Aineakas stared at them and swam at them ferociously! They were all surprised. Before they could react, she hit them one by one in the stomach. She then said, "If you don't help her out, I will make sure every day of the rest of your lives will be miserable!"

In pain, they all reluctantly agreed to help. One of them commented, "You're lucky your dad is our leader."

Coming to the rock they put over the cave, the boys whined and said, "How are we supposed to move this?"

Aineakas looked at them and responded, "You should have thought of that before you threw the rock down!" She quickly added, "I have an idea: the bottom sand where the rock has settled is soft. If we use our tails and move them back and forth while the other fish push, it would make it easier for the stone to move!"

"I'm not standing in front of that stone!" said one of the boys fearfully.

Aineakas looked at him and said, "I'll do it, you coward!" She went up front and began to move her tail back and forth vehemently. The sand spread through the water like a dust storm. The boys began to push, and I could see it begin to open.

I tried to squeeze through the top opening when all of a sudden, the boys stopped pushing and the stone clamped my tail. I cried out in agony and terror. My tail started to throb, and I involuntarily called out, "Help!" I knew Zerkalo and Aineakas were still right there trying to do everything they could to free me.

The boys swam off and Aineakas yelled at them, "You guys better hope I don't ever swim into you!" She quickly swam to the top of the stone where I was and tried to push me forward, but my tail was hurt when she pushed.

Zerkalo stood there not knowing what to do. She suggested, "Maybe we should try to remove the stone."

Aineakas looked at Zerkalo and asked, "*We?* As in you and I?"

"Yes," Zerkalo said.

Aineakas proceeded to say, "You're. . ."

Before she finished, Zerkalo piped up and asked, "I'm what? A midget fish?!?!"

Aineakas sheepishly said, "No, no... umm... I was thinking more along the lines of...you're out of your mind! Yeah! Because there's only two of us!"

"Yeah, yeah," Zerkalo responded in an irritated tone.

I spoke up, "Fish, I'm kind of in pain!"

"Oh! Yeah! Coming!" they both yelled back.

Aineakas pushed on the right side of the rock while Zerkalo moved her tail back and forth with centrifugal force. To my amazement, the rock moved, and I quickly swam out. Aineakas, who could see me, stopped pushing when she saw I was free, but Zerkalo kept going because she was covered with sand.

We both laughed and said, "You proved your point."

Hearing us laughing, she stopped and asked, "What's so funny?"

"Nothing," said Aineakas, trying to stifle her laughs.

"Come up here!" I invited her. She swam up.

Aineakas asked me, "What's your name?"

I answered, “Mar’ah.” Having already met Zerkalo, I asked, “What’s your name?”

“My name is Aineakas,” she answered.

From that point on, the three of us were friends. It did not matter to us what family we were from. So, when I looked at Aineakas, she knew what I was thinking because she saw Tsel’ and Alziwaq leave our class as well. She proceeded to blow a bubble at Zerkalo to get her attention. When the bubble hit her, it popped, and she said, “Hey!” Zerkalo turned around and saw us. We both pointed up with our right fin, and she had this expression on her face like, *“Here we go again!”*

Aineakas spoke up and said, “We would love to stay professor, but our parents all got caught in a net! And we, ummm, we,” Aineakas stammered, “have to go rescue them!” Our professor wasn’t buying it, but we quickly swam away.

“Where are we going?” Aineakas asked.

I answered, “To visit the Seers. We have to follow the sun backward.” Zerkalo looked at me as I was swimming with a dumbfounded face and I quickly answered for her, “East.”

Chapter 15

Aineakas the Healer

Aineakas

"Always remember where you come from," my dad said. "You're a Canis and a princess, Aineakas." Every time I would hear my dad say this, I would feel overwhelmed. Thoughts of failing everyone would go through my head. It was so much pressure trying to live up to the standards my dad held for me. My heart was not to rule my people, but to bring honor to them by fulfilling the prophecy. My dad however did not believe in the prophecy anymore. He was more concerned with our future and making sure his blood line ruled, unquestioned. He believed in fate.

Since I was young, I was taught how to fight. "Again!" my dad yelled as I was hit by his servant, Yahmi. Yahmi would pause. He felt pity for me as I laid there on the seafloor unable to get up from the impact that had just taken the water out of me. On the other hand, my dad had little compassion for me as I'd get hit. In fact, he'd get mad at Yahmi if he did not hit me as soon as my dad would shout out, "again." I can still hear him scolding Yahmi, "When I say 'again,' do not stop! Is that understood?"

Yahmi responded, "Yes King Zaeim."

"Get up Aineakas!" My dad screamed at me. Full of rage, I swam up and went right back into training.

All these memories went through my mind as we were headed to visit the Seers. The only reason I went to school was because my dad signed a peace treaty—a temporary one, as he would put it. Our clan was ambushed by those who serve Paragon. My mom, brothers, and sisters all perished. We lost half our clan. Although my dad would like to conquer the entire Rocky Cove, he lacks the fish to do it. So, he waited for an opportune time. He was consumed with power. I knew going on this journey meant giving up my crown, but seeing my dad consumed with power made me feel like a crown did not make you a better fish.

"Ouch!" Mar'ah screamed out.

Zerkalo and I paused and asked, "What's wrong?"

"My tail hurts," Mar'ah admitted in agony.

It was from the injury she had years ago because of being thrown in that cave. Zerkalo looked at it and told them, "That does not look good! There is no way we're going to make it. We have to turn back."

"No," Mar'ah yelled in a pain-stricken voice.

I looked at her and said, "I can help, at least I think." I swam close to her tail and said, "Don't laugh at me." I took my right fin and placed it on her tail and said nothing for a minute. Zerkalo looked at me like I was losing my mind. Then I spoke up, "You're the healer, Agape, please heal my friend." Just then Mar'ah moved her tail back and forth. To her amazement, all the pain went away.

They both looked at me in disbelief. Mar'ah spoke up, "I thought no one in your clan believed in Agape?"

I looked at her and said, "No one in my clan did believe—at least to my knowledge—until. . ." I waited a minute as we floated there and continued, "Until He found me."

"Found you?"

"Yes, He found me. My heart was seeking something and this brilliant light shone on me, and out of it came the words, 'Agape knows you.'"

Mar'ah and Zerkalo looked at Aineakas. Zerkalo asked, "How did you get the healing powers?"

I smiled and answered, "I did not get the healing powers." They both looked at me with an awkward look, and I continued, "I received Agape; healing was a byproduct of Him now living in me."

Chapter 16

A Mirror's Reflection

The Narrator

After Aineakas finished talking, the girls continued their journey. They arrived at the place that was teaming with life; there were fish of different kind everywhere, each one going about their day. The girls observed the Underwater Mountains that were covered in little tiny animals called Zooplankton. It was a wonder to see as they caused all the mountains to glow in vibrant colors. As they looked closer at the mountains, they could see snails and crabs defending their territories. Aineakas quickly snatched some snails as Mar'ah and Zerkalo grazed off one of the mountains.

Ahead of them was the abyss. Zerkalo, not sure if they should venture into the abyss, asked, "Are we going into that place?"

The girls both stopped and Mar'ah answered, "Well. . . if the boys went that way then maybe we should, too."

Zerkalo, still uncertain, asked, "What if they are all dead and we are going into a trap?"

Aineakas asked Zerkalo, "Are you scared?"

Even though she was hesitating, Zerkalo piped up loudly, "I'm not scared of anything!"

As they stood there contemplating if they should go in or not, they spotted Tsel' and Alziwaq swimming out of the Abyss and there was a look of relief on the girls' faces. As the boys swam to the girls, Aineakas spoke up, "What did you boys get yourself into?"

Tsel' responded quickly, "There is no time to explain. We have to go!"

Mar'ah assertively asked, "Where do we have to go? We deserve an explanation!"

Alziwaq and Tsel' spent the next few moments relaying the events that had transpired thus far. As soon as they mentioned *Paragon* the expression on Aineakas' face turned angry, then sad. The other fish noticed the change in her demeanor and they asked her what was wrong.

Aineakas looked at them and said, "The fish that murdered half my clan, including my mother and all of my family except my dad and I, served Paragon."

All of them were overcome with fear after hearing what Aineakas said. Zerkalo remained quiet the whole time Aineakas was telling them what had happened to her family. Even as Zerkalo exchanged glances with the rest of them, she did not speak a word. Alziwaq, at that moment, had a Word of Knowledge for Zerkalo. He looked at her and said, "You know who Paragon is, don't you?"

Zerkalo was caught off guard by the question and she quietly said, "He came to me once." She began telling her story:

"Growing up as small as I am is not easy; Tsel' can attest to just how hard it is." Tsel' nodded his head in agreement. Zerkalo continued, "I used to get beat up all the time. I would swim home after school and tell my mom and dad what was happening, but there wasn't much they could do. It's a fish eat fish world down here, if you know what I'm saying. It got so bad, that one day I spoke out in anger. I said, 'I wish I was not alive!' And I meant it! Just as those words came out of my mouth, I felt as if something dark came into my heart."

Everyone was looking intensely at Zerkalo, who had stopped talking for a moment. Mar'ah broke the silence and asked what they were all thinking, "What was it?"

Zerkalo answered, "It was Paragon." They all floated back a little as fear gripped each of their hearts. Seeing their reaction, Zerkalo quickly said, "Paragon is not there anymore!" All of them relaxed.

"Tell us what happened!" Alziwaq said eagerly.

Zerkalo went back into her story, "Paragon came in because I invited him in. I did not invite him in purposely, but ignorantly. I could hear his voice in my mind telling me I should just hurt myself. He would say, 'No one really cares about you, not even your parents! Might as well hurt yourself.' It was so tormenting; I could not sleep."

"What did you do?" Aineakas asked.

Tsel' spoke up, "Obviously she didn't do it."

"Not funny!" Mar'ah said.

"I wasn't trying to be funny," Tsel' responded in defense.

"Fish, let her finish telling the story," Alziwaq calmly said.

Zerkalo kept going, "I actually started to plan out how to hurt myself, when something happened that I was not expecting." They all moved forward in expectation of what she was about to say. "I ran into an Aphanius Mento fish named *Dóxa*. He came out of nowhere and he looked like he was in a rush to get somewhere. Yet he stopped in his

path and looked at me. His gaze was piercing, as if he could read my very thoughts.

"Dóxa introduced himself to me, then he asked me, 'Do you know what your name means?' I looked at him and slowly shook my head, 'No…' Dóxa answered, 'Your name means *mirror*.' I floated there, captivated by what he was saying. He went on and said, 'The things about mirrors is that they can reflect something beautiful or ugly. If a mirror gets placed in front of something ugly, it will stay there until it is moved. If it gets placed in front of something beautiful, it will stay there until it is moved. What do you want to reflect?'"

Zerkalo went on to tell them how she pondered Dóxa's question for several minutes, then she finally came to a standstill in her mind. She continued her story, "I told him, 'I don't know.' 'You're right,' Dóxa replied. I looked at him a bit confused by his response. He proceeded to say to me, 'You're right in the sense that you don't know the answer to the question in your mind. The purpose of the question was to reveal to you the content of your own heart. The second question is one that you must know: *What were you created to reflect?*'" Zerkalo hung her head as she remembered the encounter with Dóxa. "I didn't answer Dóxa. I just floated there, silent. As if I had no voice. Dóxa didn't judge me though. He just looked at me with compassion and said, 'Agape.' As soon as he said 'Agape,' I heard a voice in my head scream, 'No!!!' and say, 'You belong to Paragon!' Immediately, I had a migraine and felt sick to my stomach. Dóxa said, 'All you have to do is call His name and ask for His help and the torment you feel will go away.' I screamed, 'AGAPE!!! HELP!!' As soon as I said that, all the pain went away and I felt something—or rather someone—leave my body. Paragon fled when I called on Agape. From that day on, I could discern what was right and what was wrong. I could also discern what kind of spirit was behind a situation or a fish. Know this much," Zerkalo added, "I've felt the presence of Paragon and it is devoid of everything good. The fact of the matter is that it is pure evil."

Mar'ah looked at Zerkalo and asked, "Why do you think calling on Agape's name got rid of those thoughts?"

Zerkalo sat there for a second, then looked at all of them and replied, "Paragon is the father of lies. His power lies in individuals like me believing his lies. Agape, on the other hand, is the father of truth and is perfect love. Perfect love casts out all fear because fear has to do with punishment!"

As they all floated there, they were unaware that something was watching them. They were not alone. The Seers had warned the boys about the tiny creatures that serve Paragon. Unbeknownst to them, every word spoken was heard.

To be continued...

Acknowledgements

I've learned, in my life, with true friends, one can accomplish anything. I have a few people to thank for this book.

First of all, I'd like to thank my Lord and Savior, Jesus Christ! I could not have even came up with this idea if not for the inspiration of the Holy Spirit.

Secondly, my wife, who is my best friend and my number one supporter.

I could not have done this without my editor, Britani Overman. She believed in me as a writer and took a chance before anyone really ever knew I could write.

Mallory Arzola, Megan Shelby, Jacquelyn Holmes, and Jason Rutel (TheCreativeNomads.com), from the bottom of my heart, thank you!

Teri Bickford without you I don't think I could have made it to Israel. Without making it to Israel, this book could never have materialized. All that you've done for my family, I thank you. May God richly bless you!

Matthew Daniels, my brother, I could not do a lot of things without you by my side. Thank you for the amazing music you have made for this project.

Finally, Gabriella Anato. This is the beginning of your illustrative journey. I am proud of you Gabby, you help make the world a better place because of the love you have for Jesus.

Bibliography

[i] "Tristramella Simonis." Wikiwand, https://www.wikiwand.com/en/Tristramel-la_simonis.
[ii] The Editors of Encyclopaedia Britannica. "Tilapia." Encyclopædia Britannica, Encyclopædia Britannica, Inc., 29 Apr. 2011, https://www.britannica.com/animal/tilapia.
[iii] "Jesus' Gift to Peter and His Fishing Partners." Adefenceofthebiblecom, 30 Oct. 2019, https://www.adefenceofthebible.com/2019/10/30/jesus-gift-to-peter-and-his-fishing-partners/.
[iv] Brown, Driver, Briggs and Gesenius. "Hebrew Lexicon entry for Ma`an". "The NAS Old Testament Hebrew Lexicon"
[v] "What Does الزواق (Alziwaq) Mean in Arabic?" WordHippo, https://www.wordhippo.com/what-is/the-meaning-of/arabic-word-f49b982f7b42be6c22fcabb384eb08bec1c54420.html.
[vi] "What Does Цель (Tsel') Mean in Russian?" WordHippo, https://www.wordhippo.com/what-is/the-meaning-of/russian-word-e41413cd1f40844fa0bd4bda08a71764987f9ca8.html.
[vii] "PRESENT STATUS OF MASS REARING OF FRY AND FINGERLINGS IN THE EIFAC REGION." EIFAC Workshop on Mass Rearing of Fry and Fingerlings of Freshwater Fishes. Papers (1979), http://www.fao.org/3/ae993e/AE993E03.htm.
[viii] "Mar'ah - Old Testament Hebrew Lexicon - King James Version." Bible Study Tools, https://www.biblestudytools.com/lexicons/hebrew/kjv/marah.html.
[ix] "What Does Зеркало (Zerkalo) Mean in Russian?" WordHippo, https://www.wordhippo.com/what-is/the-meaning-of/russian-word-53fbab42915996423c52029cbb1823924a67db55.html.
[x] "Bioluminescent Phytoplankton: What Makes It Glow?" Google, Google, https://www.google.com/amp/s/www.leisurepro.com/blog/explore-the-blue/bioluminescent-plankton-what-makes-it-glow/amp/.

Made in the USA
Middletown, DE
31 May 2023

31580428R00042